This book belongs to:

____

a woman of prayer

Faith

When a Woman Prays
30-Day Prayer Devotional

Juanita E. Gaynor & Kiesha L. Peterson

Stella Publications, LLC

Published by Stella Publications
East Orange, NJ 07018
www.stellapublications.com
ISBN: 979-8-9862177-3-4

In Memorium

Barbara Edwards
March 13, 1946 – March 30, 2023

I can still vividly remember my aunt, who was an exceptional individual with an incredible ability to look beyond my faults and shower me with unconditional love and support. Her spirit was one of generosity and kindness, and I will forever cherish the memories of the affection and warmth she bestowed upon me.

During times of trouble or adversity, my aunt was a constant pillar of strength and encouragement. She never hesitated to offer a listening ear or a helping hand, and her unwavering love and guidance made a profound impact on my life. I am eternally grateful for the time we spent together and the incredible influence she had on my existence.

Although she has departed this world, her memory continues to resonate through the many lives she touched and the love she so generously gave. Her legacy inspires me to carry forward her spirit of compassion and kindness, and I take comfort in knowing that she will always be present in my heart and soul.

Be Joyful in hope,
Patient in affliction,
Faithful in prayer
- Romans 12:

Dedication

When A Woman Prays: 30-Day Prayer Devotion is dedicated to each and every mother, past, present, and future. Your love, strength, and devotion to your children and loved ones are immeasurable. May this prayer guide provide you with the inspiration and guidance to pray for your family's safety, health, and prosperity.

To all the mothers who have come before us, we honor your legacy and the sacrifices you made for your children. To the present mothers, we see the love and dedication you pour into your families every day. And to the future mothers, we pray that you will be blessed with the strength and wisdom to guide your children on their life's journey.

We know that as mothers, we all share the same prayer for our children and loved ones. We pray for their safety, health, and prosperity. We pray for their happiness and well-being. And we know that God hears every prayer and sees every tear that we shed.

So, to all the mothers out there, be strong and know that you are not alone. May this prayer guide be a source of comfort and inspiration to you as you continue to pray for your family's future.

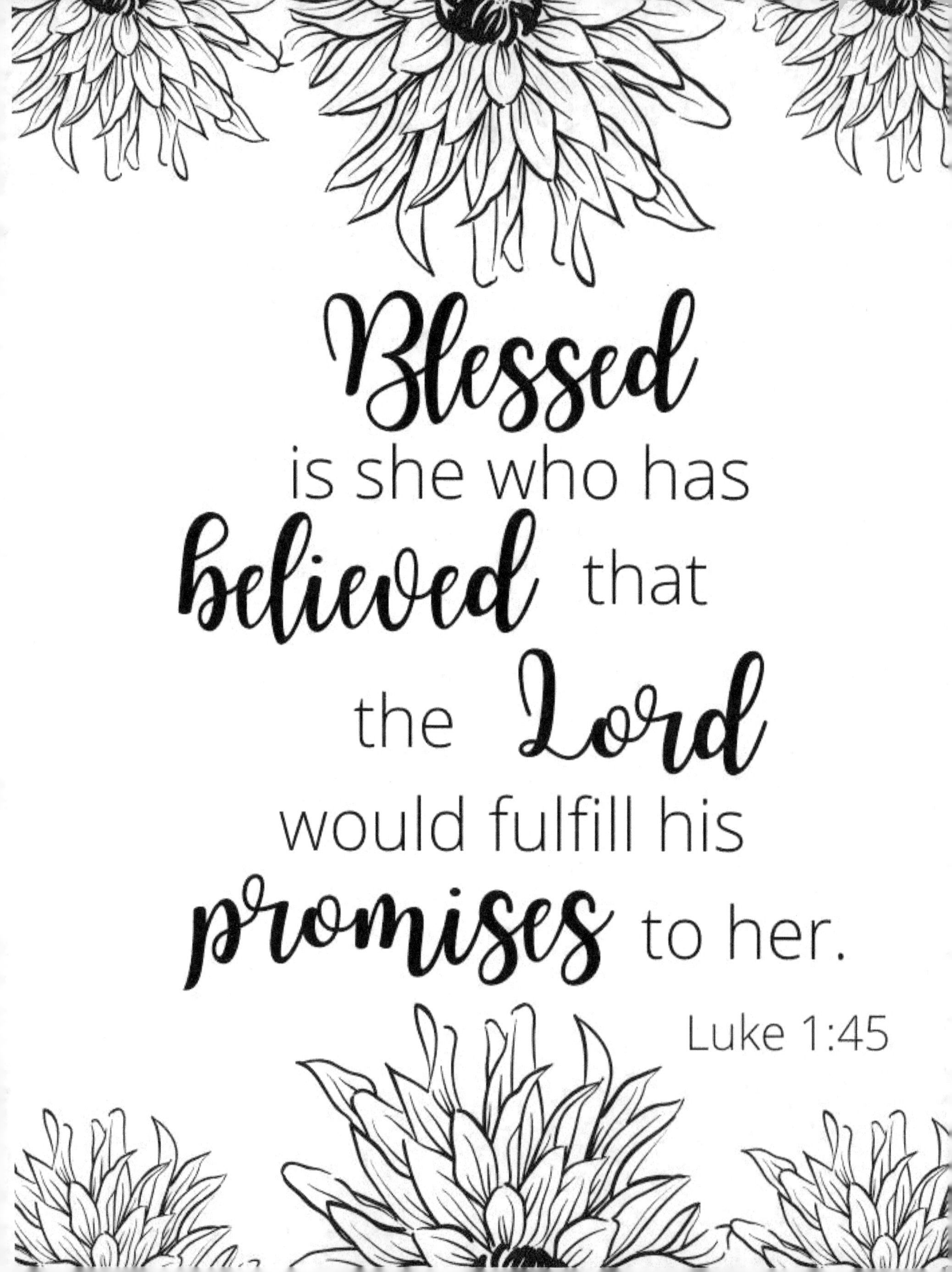

Blessed
is she who has
believed that
the Lord
would fulfill his
promises to her.
Luke 1:45

Inspiration

Elder Judith Favors and the Newark NAACP Religious Affairs Committee. When you shared the 'When A Woman Prays' event during our weekly prayer call it touched me and ignited the production of the When A Woman Prays Project. Your diligent and dedicated work to the NAACP is exemplary. I thank you for your continued support and encouragement.

worship
HEAVEN
Holy Spirit
BIBLE
cross
Faith
communion
God
salvation
PEACE
trust
SERVICE
Grace
seek
Hope
Love
Gospel
forgive
stewardship
blessings
Jesus
FELLOWSHIP
evangelism
PRAISE
act
church

From the Heart

We would like to extend our sincerest gratitude and appreciation to Dr. Marilyn E. Porter, whose unwavering dedication and commitment were indispensable to the success of this project. Without her invaluable support, this endeavor would not have been possible.

Dr. Porter's willingness to answer God's call and her remarkable leadership paved the way for our paths to intersect. She is not only our Spiritual Leader but also a cherished Sister and Friend. Her constant support, guidance, and teachings have been a continuous source of inspiration and encouragement.

Our gratitude towards Dr. Porter knows no bounds. Her contributions to this project and to our lives are immeasurable. We are forever grateful for her presence in our lives and the unwavering commitment she has shown towards our growth and development.

Foreword

As women of Christian faith, we understand the power and importance of prayer in our lives. Through prayer, we can connect with God, seek His guidance, find comfort, and experience transformation. Prayer has the ability to change our lives and the lives of those around us, and it is a powerful tool that we must utilize every day.

That is why we are excited to introduce you to our 30-Day Prayer Devotional book titled "When A Woman Prays". This devotional is designed to help women develop a prayer routine that can be life-changing. Our hope is that this devotional will not only inspire you to pray more but also deepen your relationship with God and transform your life.

Throughout the next 30 days, we will explore various aspects of prayer and how they can be applied to our daily lives. We will cover topics such as praise and worship, thanksgiving, confession, supplication, intercession, and more. Each day's devotion includes a passage of scripture, a prayer, and reflection questions that will help you to engage with the topic and apply it to your life.

One of the key things we want to emphasize in this devotional is the importance of consistency. Consistency in prayer is vital for our spiritual growth and development. When we make prayer a daily habit, we create space for God to work in our lives and align our hearts with His will.

Foreword

We understand that life can get busy and it can be challenging to carve out time for prayer. However, we want to encourage you to make prayer a priority in your life. Whether it's early in the morning, during your lunch break, or before you go to bed, find a time that works for you and make it a daily habit.

Another aspect of prayer that we want to emphasize is the power of community. While individual prayer is important, there is something special about praying together with other believers. We encourage you to find a prayer partner or a small group of women who can support you in your prayer journey. Praying together can create a sense of accountability, provide encouragement, and deepen relationships.

Ultimately, our goal with this devotional is to help women discover the power of prayer and how it can transform their lives. We believe that when we pray, we invite God into our lives and allow Him to work in and through us. Our hope is that as you journey through this devotional, you will experience the transformative power of prayer and develop a deeper, more intimate relationship with God.

We want to remind you that prayer is not just about asking God for things or telling Him what we want. It is also about surrendering our will to His and aligning ourselves with His purposes. Prayer is an opportunity to express our love and gratitude to God, to seek His guidance and wisdom, and to intercede on behalf of others.

Foreword

As you engage with this devotional, we encourage you to approach each day's topic with an open heart and mind. Allow the Holy Spirit to guide you as you reflect on the scripture, pray, and answer the reflection questions. We believe that as you do, you will experience a deeper understanding of God's love for you and His desire to work in and through your life.

In closing, we want to encourage you to approach this devotional with a sense of expectation and anticipation. Expect God to meet you where you are, to transform your heart, and to work in your life in ways you never thought possible. Anticipate the transformative power of prayer and the ways in which it will impact your life and the lives of those around you.

We are excited to journey with you through these next 30 days and look forward to seeing how God will work in and through your life as you commit to a daily prayer routine. May you be blessed, encouraged, and transformed as you seek God through prayer

Juanita E Gaynor *Kiesha L Peterson*

Introduction

When a woman prays, she engages in a spiritual practice that can provide her with numerous benefits. Prayer is a means of communication with a higher power, and it can help women to feel a sense of connection with something greater than themselves. Whether it is through reciting traditional prayers or simply speaking from the heart, prayer can be a source of comfort, strength, and inspiration.

One of the benefits of prayer for women is that it can help to reduce stress and promote emotional well-being. By taking the time to quiet the mind and focus on a higher power, women can experience a sense of inner peace and calm. This can help to reduce feelings of anxiety and depression and improve overall mental health.

In addition, prayer can be a powerful tool for personal growth and self-reflection. It allows women to reflect on their thoughts, feelings, and actions, and to gain insight into their own strengths and weaknesses. This can help them to develop a deeper understanding of themselves and their place in the world, and to cultivate greater compassion and empathy for others.

Prayer can also be a means of seeking guidance and wisdom from a higher power. Many women turn to prayer when faced with difficult decisions or challenges, and they find that it provides them with clarity and direction. By trusting in a higher power, women can feel more empowered to make positive changes in their lives and to pursue their goals and dreams.

Overall, prayer is a deeply personal and meaningful practice for many women. It can provide them with a sense of purpose and connection, and help them to navigate the challenges and complexities of life with greater ease and grace

10 benefits of Prayer

1. Prayer protects you.

2. Prayer draws you closer to God.

3. Prayer gives you hope.

4. Prayer changes things.

5. Prayer makes you happy.

6. Prayer heals you from all pain.

7. Prayer makes you less selfish.

8. Prayer makes you spiritually strong.

9. Prayer keeps you in the will of God.

10. Prayer gives you victory.

How To Do Daily Devotions Successfully

It takes a little planning to get started with daily devotions. There is no set of rules of what your devotional time will look like, but here are some step-by-step ways to be successful with your quiet time with God.

1. Pick A Place: Lying in bed with the lights off is not the best place as failure is inevitable. Finding the right place is very important for your success. Have a specific place you go to each day for your daily devotions. A comfortable chair in a quiet place in your home with a good reading light. The main thing make it work for you and your situation.

2. Pick A Time: There is no right or wrong time of day for doing devotions. Whatever time you choose, let it be the best time of day for you to have quiet time with our Savior.

3. Pick A Time Frame: Pick a time that you will be successful at. Only you know how much time realistically you can commit to each day. Recommend starting with 15 minutes and as time passes you may develop into more time. Just be realistic about your goal. If you aim too high, you will quickly get discouraged.

4. Spend Time In Prayer: Prayer is simply a two-way conversation with God. Just as you would talk to your best friend. Talk to God, tell Him about your concerns and cares, and then listen. God talks to us through His Word the Bible, through other people, through circumstances, and a still small voice.

5. Spend Time in Worship: Be thankful. God created us to praise Him. Express your praise and thankfulness in a quiet voice or out loud.

6. Writing in a Journal or Notebook: Journaling or writing in a notebook helps put your thoughts down and stay on track.

"Do not be anxious about anything, but in every situation, by prayer and petition, with thanksgiving, present your requests to God. And the peace of God, which transcends all understanding, will guard your hearts and your minds in Christ Jesus."

Philippians 4:6-7 (KJV)

"Confess your faults one to another, and pray one for another, that ye may be healed. The effectual fervent prayer of a righteous man availeth much."

James 5:16 (KJV)

Pray for Wisdom and Discernment

Scripture:

"If any of you lack wisdom, let him ask of God, that giveth to all men liberally, and upbraideth not; and it shall be given him." - James 1:5 (KJV)

Prayer

Dear Lord, Grant me the wisdom to discern your will in all things, that I may walk in the path of righteousness and avoid the snares of the enemy. Let your word be a lamp to my feet and a light to my path, that I may follow you always. Give me the courage to make difficult decisions and the humility to seek guidance when I am uncertain. May your wisdom guide my thoughts, words, and actions, today and always. Amen.

Teaching:

Prayer is the key to obtaining wisdom and discernment. In James 1:5, we are reminded that if we lack wisdom, we should ask God for it, and He will give it to us. We must have faith and trust that God will provide us with the answers we need through prayer.

Application:

Be specific in your prayers. Instead of asking for "wisdom," ask for wisdom in a particular area of your life, such as relationships, finances, or career. This will help you focus your prayers and allow God to provide more specific answers.

Reflections

Prayers
(Answered & Requested)

Praying for Spouse's Strength & Wisdom

Scripture:

"Finally, my brethren, be strong in the Lord, and in the power of his might. Put on the whole armour of God, that ye may be able to stand against the wiles of the devil." Ephesians 6:10-11 (KJV)

Prayer

Dear Lord, I lift up my spouse to you today, asking for your strength and wisdom to be upon them. May they be empowered by your grace to face every challenge and overcome every obstacle. Give them discernment to make wise decisions and courage to stand firm in their convictions. Help them to walk in your ways and follow your will for their life. Bless them with your love and favor today and always. In Jesus' name, Amen.

Teaching:

Praying for our spouse's strength and wisdom means asking God to provide them with the inner resources to face life's challenges. It displays our love and care for our partner and helps us focus on their needs. It reminds us to be supportive and encourages each other as partners in life.

Application:

To practice this teaching, set a daily prayer time for your spouse's strength and wisdom. Pray for their needs and specific guidance to support them. Remember that prayer is powerful and consistent practice strengthens your spouse.

____
____
____
____
____
____
____
____

Prayers
(Answered & Requested)

____
____
____
____
____
____
____
____

Praying for Career or Work Success

Scripture:

"Be careful for nothing; but in everything by prayer and supplication with thanksgiving let your requests be made known unto God. And the peace of God, which passeth all understanding, shall keep your hearts and minds through Christ Jesus." Philippians 4:6-7 (KJV)

Prayer

Dear God, I come before you today seeking your guidance and blessing in my career. Help me to use the talents and skills you have given me to the best of my ability, and may my work be pleasing to you. Give me wisdom to make sound decisions, perseverance to overcome challenges, and favor with those I work with. May my work bring glory to your name and be a source of blessing to others. In Jesus' name, Amen.

Teaching:

To pray for career success, know that God wants us to succeed using our gifts to glorify Him. Seek His guidance and trust Him to provide opportunities. Work hard, be diligent, and trust that God honors our efforts. Success is ultimately in His hands.

Application:

To apply these teachings, commit to a daily prayer routine focused on work success. Thank God for gifts, ask Him to guide you, and be specific. Seek His guidance, work hard, and give thanks for opportunities and successes. Always give Him the glory for achievements in your career.

Reflections

Prayers
(Answered & Requested)

Praying for Complete Health

Scripture:

"Beloved, I wish above all things that thou mayest prosper and be in health, even as thy soul prospereth." - 3 John 1:2 (KJV)

Prayer

Dear Lord, I come to you today seeking complete health and healing in my body. You are the Great Physician, and I trust in your power to restore me to full health. I pray that you will remove all sickness, pain, and disease from my body and strengthen me in every way. Help me to honor you with my body and to use my renewed health to serve others and bring glory to your name. In Jesus' name, Amen.

Teaching:

As believers, we can focus on prayer for our health, as God desires us to be healthy in body, mind, and spirit. Prayer is powerful and can bring healing and guidance. Just as we care for our spiritual health, we should care for our physical and mental health through prayer and healthy practices.

Application:

Reflect on your health status and commit to daily prayer for complete health, seeking God's guidance in caring for body, mind, and spirit. Adopt healthy lifestyle changes such as nutrition, rest, and exercise, trusting that God will bless your efforts and help you thrive in all areas of life.

Reflections

Prayers
(Answered & Requested)

Praying for Fearless Calm

Scripture:

"I sought the Lord, and he heard me, and delivered me from all my fears." - Psalm 34:4 (KJV)

Prayer

Dear God, I come to you today asking for your help in overcoming fear and anxiety. Please fill me with your peace, which surpasses all understanding, and calm my anxious thoughts. Help me to trust in your perfect love that casts out all fear. May I be confident in your presence and know that you are always with me, guiding and protecting me. Strengthen me to face every challenge with fearless calm. In Jesus' name, Amen.

Teaching:

In this scripture, we see the psalmist declaring their trust in the Lord to deliver them from all their fears. When we seek the Lord in prayer, we can also experience the same kind of deliverance from fear. Fear and anxiety can be paralyzing, but as we turn to God and place our trust in Him, He can calm our hearts and bring us a sense of peace.

Application:

Remember that praying for fearless calm is not a one-time event, but a continual process. As we surrender our fears to God, He can transform them into opportunities for growth and deeper trust in Him. Make it a priority to spend time in prayer each day, inviting God's peace to fill your heart and mind.

Reflections

____

____

____

____

____

____

____

Prayers
(Answered & Requested)

____

____

____

____

____

____

____

____

Praying for Our Country's Leaders

Scripture:

"I exhort therefore, that, first of all, supplications, prayers, intercessions, and giving of thanks, be made for all men; For kings, and for all that are in authority; that we may lead a quiet and peaceable life in all godliness and honesty." - 1 Timothy 2:1-2 (KJV)

Prayer

Dear Lord, I lift up our country's leaders to you today, asking for your wisdom and guidance to be upon them. Grant them discernment to make wise decisions that honor you and serve the common good. May they lead with humility and seek the well-being of all people, especially the most vulnerable. Give them strength to overcome obstacles and courage to stand for truth and justice. Bless our nation with your peace and prosperity. In Jesus' name, Amen.

Teaching:

We must pray for our country's leaders to align with God's will, acknowledging that He can work through them for positive change. Our prayers have a significant impact on their lives and decision-making.

Application:

Take time each day to pray for our country's leaders. Pray for them to have wisdom, discernment, and courage to make decisions that honor God and benefit the people they serve. Ask God to work through them to bring about positive change in our country, and trust that He will answer your prayers according to His perfect will.

Reflections

Prayers
(Answered & Requested)

Praying for Church Needs

Scripture:

"And let us consider one another to provoke unto love and to good works: Not forsaking the assembling of ourselves together, as the manner of some is; but exhorting one another: and so much the more, as ye see the day approaching." - Hebrews 10:24-25 (KJV)

Prayer

Dear God, I come to you today lifting up the needs of our church community. We pray for your provision for every need and that you would bless our church with the resources to carry out your mission. We ask for your guidance and wisdom as we seek to minister to those in our community and spread the good news of your love. May our church be a beacon of hope and a source of healing to all who enter our doors. In Jesus' name, Amen.

Teaching:

Praying for our church and its needs seeks God's provision, guidance, and protection for the community of believers. Through prayer, the church can experience positive change, unity, and fulfill its purpose in serving and glorifying God, demonstrating our love and commitment to His people.

Application:

Form a habit of praying regularly for your church's leadership, congregation, and any specific needs or challenges it may face. Ask for God's provision, guidance, and protection and find ways to serve and support your church.

Reflections

____
____
____
____
____
____
____

Prayers
(Answered & Requested)

____
____
____
____
____
____
____
____

Praying for Purposeful Service

Scripture:

"As every man hath received the gift, even so minister the same one to another, as good stewards of the manifold grace of God." - 1 Peter 4:10 (KJV)

Prayer

Dear God, I pray that you would guide me to serve you and others with purpose and passion. Help me to use the gifts and talents you have given me to make a meaningful impact in the lives of those around me. May my service be a reflection of your love and grace, and may it bring glory to your name. Lead me to opportunities to serve and inspire me to make a difference in the world. In Jesus' name, Amen.

Teaching:

God has given each of us unique spiritual gifts, talents, and abilities that we can use to serve others and bring Him glory. When we pray for purposeful service, we're asking God to reveal our gifts and show us how we can use them to make a difference in the world. Through service, we fulfill our purpose and bless others.

Application:

Consider your gifts, pray for guidance on using them to serve and glorify God. Look for opportunities to serve in your community and church. Every act of service, no matter how small, can make a big difference in someone's life.

____

____

____

____

____

____

____

Prayers
(Answered & Requested)

____

____

____

____

____

____

____

____

____

Praying for Global Suffering and Pain

Scripture:

"And the King shall answer and say unto them, Verily I say unto you, Inasmuch as ye have done it unto one of the least of these my brethren, ye have done it unto me." – Matthew 25:40 (KJV)

Prayer

Heavenly Father, we come to you with heavy hearts for the suffering and pain of our global family. We ask for your mercy and love to heal their bodies, minds, and spirits. Show us how to be your hands and feet, and serve those in need practically. May our actions and prayers bring comfort, hope, and light to dark places. We trust in your sovereignty and love, and lift our world to you. Amen.

Teaching:

As Christians, it is our duty to show compassion and love towards those who are suffering, whether it be physical, emotional, or spiritual pain. When we pray for those who are hurting around the world, we are not only showing them that they are not alone, but we are also fulfilling our duty to serve Christ.

Application:

Create a prayer list of those in need globally. Use it during personal prayer or with a group of committed believers. Donate to charities or volunteer to serve those in need for a practical impact.

Reflections

____

____

____

____

____

____

____

Prayers
(Answered & Requested)

____

____

____

____

____

____

____

____

Praying for Your Future Aspirations

Scripture:

"Commit thy works unto the Lord, and thy thoughts shall be established."
- Proverbs 16:3 (KJV)

Prayer

Heavenly Father, guide my aspirations and help me align my goals with Your perfect plan. I commit my plans to You and seek Your wisdom and strength to pursue my dreams. Thank You for being my faithful companion on this journey. In Jesus' name, I pray. Amen.

Teaching:

As believers, we are called to commit our plans and aspirations to the Lord in prayer. When we surrender our plans to God and seek His guidance, He can establish our thoughts and lead us in the right direction. Prayer is a powerful tool that can help us align our hearts with God's will and bring clarity to our goals and aspirations.

Application:

Dedicate daily time to pray and seek God's guidance. Keep a prayer journal to reflect on your goals and their alignment with God's plan. Ask for His will and wisdom to pursue it. Trust His timing and direction above your own.

Reflections

____

____

____

____

____

____

____

Prayers
(Answered & Requested)

____

____

____

____

____

____

____

Praying for Unconditional Love & Forgiveness

Scripture:

"For if ye forgive men their trespasses, your heavenly Father will also forgive you: But if ye forgive not men their trespasses, neither will your Father forgive your trespasses." – Matthew 6:14-15 (KJV)

Prayer

Heavenly Father, I come to You today to pray for the gift of unconditional love and forgiveness. Help me to see others through Your eyes, to understand their perspective, and to extend grace and forgiveness to them. Fill me with Your love, which surpasses all understanding, and enable me to love others as You love me. Thank You for Your mercy and forgiveness towards me. In Jesus' name, I pray. Amen.

Teaching:

Forgiveness and unconditional love are crucial aspects of Christianity. Forgiveness is not optional, and it's necessary to receive God's forgiveness. Forgiving others may be challenging, but it's not about excusing their actions. Instead, it frees us from negative emotions like anger and bitterness.

Application:

When struggling to forgive, pray for the person. Ask God to help you see them as He does and fill you with His love. Forgiveness takes time, but receiving God's love helps extend it to others. Seek reconciliation with the person, building a relationship based on forgiveness, grace, and love.

Reflections

____
____
____
____
____
____
____

Prayers
(Answered & Requested)

____
____
____
____
____
____
____
____

Praying for Unwavering, Steadfast Faith

Scripture:

"Watch ye, stand fast in the faith, quit you like men, be strong."
- 1 Corinthians 16:13 (KJV)

Prayer

Dear God, strengthen me with Your mighty power, that I may be rooted and grounded in Your love. Help me understand the depth of Your love, surpassing knowledge. Fill me with Your fullness and keep me steadfast in my faith. In Jesus' name, Amen.

Teaching:

Christians must pray for unwavering, steadfast faith as Satan seeks to steal and the world distracts. Pray for God's strength to withstand trials and comprehend His love, as He grants the power to be rooted in love and filled with the fullness of God.

Application:

To pray for unwavering faith, prioritize daily prayer and Bible reading, asking God for discipline and desire. Read, reflect and pray for strength. Connect with fellow believers to grow and stand firm in faith amidst trials.

Reflections

Prayers
(Answered & Requested)

Praying For Clarity Amidst Doubts In Faith

Scripture:

"Trust in the Lord with all thine heart; and lean not unto thine own understanding. In all thy ways acknowledge him, and he shall direct thy paths." - Proverbs 3:5-6 (KJV)

Prayer

Heavenly Father, in moments of doubt and uncertainty, we come to you seeking clarity and guidance. Help us to trust in your wisdom and understanding, and not lean on our own understanding. We surrender our doubts to you and ask for your direction in our lives. Fill us with your peace and assurance and grant us the strength to continue to seek your truth. In Jesus' name, we pray. Amen.

Teaching:

In doubt, remember you're not alone. Ask God for guidance; trust Him, not yourself. Surrender doubts and let God direct your path. Pray for clarity; receive the answers you need. Trust in the Lord. Embrace prayer as a powerful tool to communicate with God, seek His wisdom, and find peace amidst uncertainty. Let faith guide you.

Application:

Amidst doubt, pray for clarity, trust that God will provide the guidance and direction you need. Make prayer a daily routine and seek help from your faith community. Remember, seeking understanding is a journey, be patient.

Reflections

Prayers
(Answered & Requested)

Praying For Healthy Relationships

Scripture:

"And be ye kind one to another, tenderhearted, forgiving one another, even as God for Christ's sake hath forgiven you." - Ephesians 4:32 (KJV)

Prayer

Dear God, please help us to cultivate healthy relationships with those around us. May we learn to extend kindness, compassion, and forgiveness to others, just as You have shown us. Give us the strength to communicate openly and honestly, actively listen, and seek to understand one another. Help us to establish healthy boundaries where needed and surround ourselves with people who uplift and support us. We trust in You to guide us on this journey. Amen.

Teaching:

Praying for healthy relationships is essential for a fulfilling life. It involves expressing kindness, compassion, and forgiveness to others, just as Christ has forgiven us. We must also be willing to communicate openly and honestly, actively listen, and seek to understand others. Additionally, it's important to set healthy boundaries and surround ourselves with people who uplift and support us.

Application:

Set time each day to pray for relationships. Ask God for grace, forgiveness, and strength to set boundaries. Practice active listening, seek understanding, evaluate and distance from toxic or draining relationships. Seek positivity and encouragement.

Reflections

____

____

____

____

____

____

____

Prayers
(Answered & Requested)

____

____

____

____

____

____

____

Praying For Clarity On Unanswered Prayers

Scripture:

"And all things, whatsoever ye shall ask in prayer, believing, ye shall receive."
- Matthew 21:22 (KJV)

Prayer

Dear Heavenly Father, I come to you today seeking clarity on unanswered prayers in my life. I trust in Your perfect timing and plan for my life, but I also ask for the wisdom and discernment to understand Your will. Help me to have faith that You hear my prayers and that You are working behind the scenes, even when I can't see it. Thank You for Your love, grace, and provision in my life. Amen.

Teaching:

Prayer is communication with God where we express our desires, needs, and concerns. Unanswered prayers may lead us to question God's listening, but His timing is not ours, and answers may come in unexpected ways. Praying for clarity requires faith that God hears and is working, and we must approach our prayers with an open heart and mind.

Application:

Take time each day to pray and meditate on unanswered prayers. Be specific in requests, but open to God's guidance. Ask for wisdom and discernment to understand His will and trust in His timing. Stay alert for signs and opportunities as they may be answers in unexpected ways. Give thanks for God's love, grace, and provision.

Reflections

____

____

____

____

____

____

____

Prayers
(Answered & Requested)

____

____

____

____

____

____

____

____

Praying for Our Families

Scripture:

"Behold, children are a heritage from the Lord, the fruit of the womb a reward. Like arrows in the hand of a warrior are the children of one's youth. Blessed is the man who fills his quiver with them!" - Psalm 127:3-5 (KJV)

Prayer

Dear Lord, we come to you with humble hearts, asking for your love and guidance to bless our family. Please give us the strength to love and support each other, even in times of struggle. Help us to prioritize spending time together and growing in our faith. We pray for your protection over our family and for wisdom to make good decisions. Thank you for the gift of family and for your never-ending love. Amen.

Teaching:

Prayer is not just about asking for things. While it's okay to ask God for our needs, prayer is also about worship, confession, thanksgiving, and intercession. When we pray, we should take the time to acknowledge God's greatness, confess our sins, express our gratitude, and pray for others.

Application:

Keep a prayer journal. Create a family prayer time. Encourage each family member to keep a prayer journal where they can write down their prayer requests, praises, and answers to prayer. This will help them see how God is working in their lives and build their faith. Pray without ceasing.

Reflections

Prayers
(Answered & Requested)

Praying For Your Friend's Needs

Scripture:

"Confess your faults one to another, and pray one for another, that ye may be healed. The effectual fervent prayer of a righteous man availeth much."- James 5:16 (KJV)

Prayer

Dear Heavenly Father, I come to you today on behalf of my dear friend. Lord, you know their needs better than anyone else, and I ask that you meet them in their time of need. Please provide comfort, healing, and strength where it is needed. Give them guidance, wisdom, and direction in their decisions. May your peace and love surround them, and may they feel your presence every day. In Jesus' name, Amen.

Teaching:

Pray with Faith and Belief - When you pray, you should do so with faith and belief that God is listening and will answer your prayers. Believe that God is capable of working in your friend's life and that your prayers can make a difference.

Application:

Make a List of Prayer Requests - Consider making a list of prayer requests for your friends so you can keep track of their needs. This will help you stay organized and ensure that you don't forget to pray for something important.

Reflections

____

____

____

____

____

____

____

Prayers
(Answered & Requested)

____

____

____

____

____

____

____

____

Praying For Your Finances

Scripture:

"But seek ye first the kingdom of God, and his righteousness; and all these things shall be added unto you."
Matthew 6:33 (KJV)

Prayer

Heavenly Father, I come to you with a grateful heart and ask for your provision in my finances. Please bless my efforts and guide me towards opportunities that will bring prosperity and abundance. Help me to manage my finances wisely and to use them in ways that honor you. I trust in your loving care and believe that you will provide all that I need. Thank you for your faithfulness. Amen.

Teaching:

Pray for wisdom and guidance in managing your finances. God desires for us to be good stewards of the resources He has given us, and He is always willing to provide us with the wisdom we need to make sound financial decisions.

Application:

Seek out and follow wise financial advice, while also seeking God's guidance through Prayer. Consult with financial experts and read books on personal finance, but also ask God to direct your steps and show you the right path to take. Trust in His provision as you work towards your financial goals.

Reflections

Prayers
(Answered & Requested)

Praying For Forgiveness

Scripture:

"For if ye forgive men their trespasses, your heavenly Father will also forgive you: But if ye forgive not men their trespasses, neither will your Father forgive your trespasses."

Matthew 6:14-15 (KJV)

Prayer

Dear Lord, I humbly come before you, asking for your forgiveness for my sins. I acknowledge that I have fallen short and ask for your mercy and grace. Please cleanse me of all unrighteousness and renew a right spirit within me. Help me to walk in your ways and lead a life that honors you. Thank you for your unconditional love and forgiveness. In Jesus' name, Amen.

Teaching:

Grace is the foundation of forgiveness and the unmerited favor of God. We must remember that we are not worthy of God's forgiveness, but it is only by His grace that we are forgiven. When we pray, we should ask God for grace to help us forgive ourselves and others.

Application:

As a woman of Christian faith, forgiveness is an important aspect of my beliefs. Forgiveness frees us from bitterness and resentment and brings peace to our hearts. To forgive is to release someone from the debt they owe us. Let us forgive as we have been forgiven.

Reflections

Prayers
(Answered & Requested)

Praying for Our Local Community's Needs

Scripture:

"Pray without ceasing."
1 Thessalonians 5:17 (KJV)

Prayer

Dear God, we come to you with humble hearts, asking for your guidance and support for our community. We pray for those who are struggling with poverty, sickness, and despair. We ask that you bless our local leaders with wisdom and courage to make decisions that will benefit all of us. May your love and compassion be felt by all in need. We trust in your provision and thank you for your unfailing grace. Amen.

Teaching:

Praying for our community is an act of love and compassion. It requires us to humble ourselves and acknowledge our dependence on God. We should pray for our leaders, neighbors, and all those in need. Through Prayer, we can ask God to heal and restore our community.

Application:

When you pray focus on God's will instead of your own desires. Ask Him to help you discern His will for your life and give you the strength and courage to follow it. Keep a Prayer journal to track your Prayers, reflect on God's answers, and record insights or revelations that you receive.

Reflections

Prayers
(Answered & Requested)

Praying For Missionaries Spreading The Gospel

Scripture:

"brethren, pray for us, that the word of the lord may have free course, and be glorified, even as it is with you."
2 Thessalonians 3:1 (KJV)

Prayer

Dear God, we lift up our missionaries who have dedicated their lives to spreading your Gospel. Grant them your protection, and guidance as they share the message of your love and salvation with those who have not yet heard it. Give them strength and courage to face obstacles that come their way. May they be filled with your Holy Spirit and be effective witnesses of your grace and truth. In Jesus' name, we pray. Amen.

Teaching:

Prayer is a powerful tool that can transform lives and situations. When we pray, we are acknowledging our dependence on God and asking for His guidance. Through Prayer, we can also intercede for others, and God can work through our Prayers to bring about miraculous changes in people's lives.

Application:

Use Prayer to connect with others and build relationships. As missionaries, you may encounter people who are skeptical or resistant to the gospel. By praying for them and showing them kindness and compassion, you can demonstrate the love of Christ and create opportunities for God to work in their lives.

Reflections

Prayers
(Answered & Requested)

Praying for Your Faith's Growth & Development

Scripture:

"But grow in grace, and in the knowledge of our Lord and Saviour Jesus Christ. To him be glory both now and forever. Amen."
2 Peter 3:18 (KJV)

Prayer

Dear God, I come before you with a humble heart, asking that you would guide me in my faith's growth and development. Help me to deepen my understanding of your word and to live out your Teaching in my daily life. Grant me the courage and strength to overcome any obstacles that may come my way, and may my faith continue to flourish and bear fruit. In Jesus' name, I pray. Amen.

Teaching:

Prayer is a powerful tool for personal growth and development in faith. It is a way of communicating with God and opening up to His guidance and wisdom. Developing a consistent Prayer routine can help deepen our relationship with God and feel more connected to Him throughout our daily lives.

Application:

Set aside time for quiet reflection and meditation. Find a quiet place where you can focus your mind and heart on God and spend a few moments each day in quiet reflection and meditation. This can help you feel more centered and connected to God throughout the day.

Reflections

Prayers
(Answered & Requested)

Praying For Resolution In Relationship Conflicts

Scripture:

"Confess your faults one to another, and pray one for another, that ye may be healed. The effectual fervent prayer of a righteous man availeth much."- James 5:16 (KJV)

Prayer

Dear God, I come before you with a humble heart, asking that you would guide me in my faith's growth and development. Help me to deepen my understanding of your word and to live out your Teaching in my daily life. Grant me the courage and strength to overcome any obstacles that may come my way, and may my faith continue to flourish and bear fruit. In Jesus' name, I pray. Amen.

Teaching:

When we pray, we must approach God with a humble and contrite heart, confessing our own faults and shortcomings. This not only helps us to become more aware of our own faults but also helps us to see the situation from the other person's perspective and develop empathy towards them.

Application:

The first application is to set aside time for Prayer daily, both individually and with the person or people you are in conflict with. During this time, ask God for wisdom and guidance, and pray for healing and restoration in your relationships.

Reflections

____

____

____

____

____

____

____

Prayers
(Answered & Requested)

____

____

____

____

____

____

____

____

Praying For Peace In Your Heart & World

Scripture:

"Be careful for nothing; but in everything by Prayer and supplication with thanksgiving let your requests be made known unto God. And the peace of God, which passeth all understanding, shall keep your hearts and minds through Christ Jesus." - Philippians 4:6-7 (KJV)

Prayer

Loving God, I come to you today overflowing with gratitude. I thank you for the countless blessings in my life. You have given me the gift of life, good health, a loving family, supportive friends, and opportunities beyond measure. Your love and grace have been my foundation, giving me strength through every challenge. May I always be mindful to give thanks in every circumstance and focus on your goodness. Thank you for your generosity. Amen.

Teaching:

To find peace through Prayer, we should practice gratitude and thanksgiving. According to scripture, we should express our requests to God with thanksgiving. By concentrating on the things we appreciate, we can redirect our attention from our troubles to God's benevolence, which can bring us peace and contentment during challenging times.

Application:

In addition to bringing your concerns to God, make a conscious effort to focus on gratitude and thanksgiving throughout your day. This could involve keeping a gratitude journal, taking time to thank God for specific blessings, or simply pausing throughout your day to appreciate the beauty of God's creation.

Reflections

____
____
____
____
____
____
____
____

Prayers
(Answered & Requested)

____
____
____
____
____
____
____
____
____

Praying for Endurance in Your Trials

Scripture:

"And whatsoever ye shall ask in my name, that will I do, that the Father may be glorified in the Son."
John 14:13 (KJV)

Prayer

Lord, I come before you in the midst of my trials and struggles. I ask for your strength and endurance to persevere through these difficult times. Help me to keep my faith and trust in you, knowing that you are with me always. Grant me the wisdom to learn from these experiences and the courage to face whatever challenges lie ahead. Thank you for your unfailing love and mercy. In Jesus' name, I pray. Amen.

Teaching:

Another important aspect of Prayer is to pray with faith. In James, it says that if we ask for something in Prayer but doubt in our hearts, we will not receive it (James 1:6-7). It is important to pray with confidence and trust in God's ability to answer our Prayers.

Application:

Develop a Prayer routine and habitually pray in Jesus' name. Acknowledge Jesus' authority and power in your life at the beginning of your Prayers. Focus on having faith and trust in God's ability to answer your Prayers, rather than worrying or doubting. Approach God with a heart full of faith.

Reflections

____

____

____

____

____

____

____

Prayers
(Answered & Requested)

____

____

____

____

____

____

____

Praying For Effective Communication With Others

Scripture:

"Be careful for nothing; but in everything by Prayer and supplication with thanksgiving let your requests be made known unto God. And the peace of God, which passeth all understanding, shall keep your hearts and minds through Christ Jesus." - Philippians 4:6-7 (KJV)

Prayer

God, please grant me the ability to communicate effectively with others. Help me to listen with an open heart and mind, and to speak with clarity and kindness. May my words be thoughtful, and respectful. May I always seek to understand the perspectives of those around me. Grant me the patience and empathy to navigate difficult conversations with grace and wisdom. May my interactions with others be a reflection of your love and grace. Amen.

Teaching:

Prayer is the foundation for effective communication with others. Just as we need to listen and speak thoughtfully to connect with others, we must approach Prayer with the same intentionality. Being present in our conversations with God opens our hearts and minds to receive His guidance, which can shape our interactions with others.

Application:

Pray for the people you will communicate with, asking God to give you the right words and a heart to connect with them meaningfully. Practice active listening, seeking to understand their perspectives and needs. Listen for God's voice during Prayer. This will help build stronger relationships and communicate more effectively.

____

____

____

____

____

____

____

Prayers
(Answered & Requested)

____

____

____

____

____

____

____

____

Praying for Your Self-Confidence and Esteem

Scripture:

"Let us, therefore, come boldly unto the throne of grace, that we may obtain mercy, and find grace to help in time of need."
Hebrews 4:16 (KJV)

Prayer

Dear God, I come to you with a humble heart and ask for your guidance in building my self-confidence and self-esteem. Help me to believe in myself and my abilities, and to trust that I am capable of achieving my dreams. May I have the courage to step out of my comfort zone and take risks, knowing that I am worthy and deserving of success. Thank you for your love and support. Amen.

Teaching:

God desires us to come to Him with confidence in Prayer. This means we don't have to doubt or fear when we approach Him, but instead, we can have faith that He hears us and will answer us according to His will.

Application:

Use scripture and affirmations to reinforce our identity in Christ. For example, repeat phrases like "I am loved by God," "I am fearfully and wonderfully made," or "I am a child of God." This can help build our self-esteem and confidence in Prayer.

Reflections

Prayers
(Answered & Requested)

Praying For Patience To Wait On God

Scripture:

"But they that wait upon the Lord shall renew their strength; they shall mount up with wings as eagles; they shall run, and not be weary; and they shall walk, and not faint."
Isaiah 40:31 (KJV)

Prayer

Dear God, grant me the patience to wait on you. In this fast-paced world, it's easy to become restless and anxious, but I know that your timing is perfect. Help me to trust in your plan and to find peace in the waiting. Give me the strength to endure the challenges that may arise during this time and to grow closer to you in the process. Thank you for your unwavering love and guidance. Amen.

Teaching:

One aspect of developing patience and waiting on God's timing in Prayer is having faith that God is in control and has a plan for our lives. It may be tempting to take matters into our own hands and try to force outcomes. It's important to trust in God's timing.

Application:

Finally, it's important to seek support and encouragement from other believers in our faith community. By sharing our Prayer requests and journey with others, we can find comfort and strength in knowing that we're not alone in our struggles, and can draw inspiration and guidance from others' experiences and perspectives.

Reflections

Prayers
(Answered & Requested)

Praying for Overcoming Addictions & Struggles

Scripture:

"Confess your faults one to another, and pray one for another, that ye may be healed. The effectual fervent Prayer of a righteous man availeth much."
James 5:16 (KJV)

Prayer

Dear Lord, we pray for those struggling with addictions and other challenges. We ask that you guide them towards the strength and courage needed to overcome their struggles. Please give them the faith and hope to believe in themselves and trust in your divine guidance. Grant them the grace to resist temptation and to persevere through the trials of life. May they find comfort in your love and the support of those around them. Amen.

Teaching:

Prayer is powerful. James teaches us that the effectual fervent Prayer of a righteous person avails much. This means that Prayers have the power to make a difference in our lives and the lives of others and is a powerful tool that we can use to overcome addictions and struggles

Application:

Confession: Take time to confess your faults to God and to someone you trust. This could be a pastor, a counselor, or a friend.
Intercession: Pray diligently for others.
Fervency: Develop a consistent Prayer routine and be fervent in your Prayers. Set aside time each day to pray intentionally.

Reflections

Prayers
(Answered & Requested)

Praying for Gratitude and Blessings

Scripture:

"Enter into his gates with thanksgiving, and into his courts with praise: be thankful unto him, and bless his name."
Psalm 100:4 (KJV)

Prayer

Dear divine source of all blessings, I come before you with a heart full of gratitude for all the blessings I have received. Thank you for the gift of life, for the love of family and friends, for the opportunities that have come my way, and for the challenges that have helped me grow. May I never take these blessings for granted and always remember to acknowledge them with humility and gratitude. Amen.

Teaching:

Dear divine source of all blessings, I come before you with a heart full of gratitude for all the blessings I have received. Thank you for the gift of life, for the love of family and friends, for the opportunities that have come my way, and for the challenges that have helped me grow. May I never take these blessings for granted and always remember to acknowledge them with humility and gratitude. Amen.

Application:

Share your gratitude with others. When we are grateful, we naturally want to share our blessings with others. Take time to express your gratitude to people in your life who have made a difference. This practice not only helps us cultivate a spirit of gratitude but also strengthens our relationships.

Reflections

Prayers
(Answered & Requested)

Personal Notes

Personal Notes

Personal Notes

Personal Notes

Personal Notes

Personal Notes

About the Authors

Juanita is a successful entrepreneur and bestselling author based in New Jersey. Originally from Philadelphia, Juanita holds degrees in Business Administration and Accounting and has founded and currently operates five companies including EABJ Consulting and Event Management, Elite Financial Management, Restored 2 Life Ministries, Stella Publications LLC, and Stella Notary Services.

In addition to her impressive business acumen, Juanita is also a multi-talented creative with a passion for music and cooking. She is the host and producer of the Moving Past You Radio Show and the co-author of three inspiring books: I Am Who God Says I Am: Living My Life on Purpose, 100 Words of Inspiration, and It's ME Oh Lord: Early Morning Devotions.

Juanita's ultimate goal is to be a beacon of light in the world, always living out the purpose that God has for her. She credits her success in business and in life to her willingness to be open and guided by her faith. With a global expansion of her companies in the works, Juanita is poised to continue making a positive impact on the world.

Kiesha L. Peterson, a self-published author, motivational speaker, and minister with a passion for empowering others. Kiesha is a proud mother of three and grandmother of six who has dedicated her life to helping people find their purpose and live fulfilling lives. Kiesha is the founder and CEO of Absolute Word Ministries and GC Peterson Publishing. She has written and self-published four books, all of which have become bestsellers on Amazon and internationally. Her first anthology, I Am Who God Says I Am: Living My Life On Purpose, was published on her 50th birthday in 2019, and she has contributed to various magazines such as Women's Frontline Magazine and Victorious, Virtuous, and Valued Magazine.

In addition to her writing, Kiesha is a motivational speaker, using her powerful message of INpowerment™ to inspire and uplift audiences across the country. She is also a self-publishing coach, helping aspiring authors bring their own stories to life.

Kiesha is an active member of her community, and is a proud member of the Women's Speaker Association and attends Church of the New Covenant. With her dedication to empowering others, Kiesha continues to make a positive impact on the world, one book and one speech at a time.